自己的快樂
自己找

文／孟瑛如
圖／林慧婷
英文翻譯／吳侑達

大貓熊天天總是很不快樂！

因為他覺得為什麼全世界都搞不清楚他的名字，一下叫他「大熊貓」，一下叫他「大貓熊」，這讓他覺得很煩！很火大！

為什麼貓熊族群的生育率如此低呢？再這樣下去，他們可能不只是被稱為「生物界的活化石」，而是真的要成為化石了！

所以天天有時會拔自己的毛，有時亂摔東西，或者對爸媽大吼大叫，想發洩一下！

但他還是常常覺得很不快樂！這天，他決定到外面走一走。

走著走著，天天看到一隻黑熊正靠著樹幹磨自己的背，舒服到瞇起眼睛大叫著：「啊～真的好舒服、好快樂！」旁邊還有兩隻在泥塘裡打滾的野豬，用圓滾滾的身體在泥水裡滾來滾去，嘴都笑得幾乎裂到耳根後嚷嚷著：「哈哈哈，好棒、好快樂！」

　　天天不明白他們為什麼會這麼快樂，忍不住問：「你們為什麼這麼快樂呢？」黑熊和野豬異口同聲的說：「做自己喜歡的事就會快樂呀！」

蜜蜂也飛過來湊熱鬧說：「吃自己喜歡的東西也會很快樂！你看啊，我在找我最喜歡的花粉和花蜜，同時又幫忙了花朵授粉，像這樣幫助別人也可以很快樂喔！」

於是天天學著他們，舒服的倒在岩石上，一面緩慢磨背，一面豪邁的啃竹子，連嘴邊掉下來的竹子渣渣灑滿毛茸茸的肚皮也不管了。岩石上原本有隻烏龜在休息，因為天天突然出現而嚇得滾到岩石下翻不了身，天天看見了，就用胖胖的手順便幫忙烏龜翻了個身。

看著烏龜感激的臉，天天想起蜜蜂說的：「幫助別人也可以很快樂喔！」覺得自己做了喜歡的事，吃了喜歡的東西，舉手之勞幫忙解決了問題，快樂好像真的一點一滴降臨了……

天天問烏龜：「你走得這麼慢，為什麼還要出來走動呢？」

烏龜扭扭自己剛才因跌倒而有點歪掉的殼說：「走得慢還是要走，因為運動可以讓我快樂！」在旁邊蹦跳的野兔也附和著說：「運動真的可以帶來快樂，你看我有多快樂！」

天天的腦海裡浮現出自己每天規律運動後，身材變得凹凸有致的畫面，再加上剛才吃了不少竹子，正覺得好撐，於是開始跟著野兔蹦跳，繞著烏龜快走，覺得快樂好像在心裡一點一滴慢慢積蓄了起來。

天天在藍天白雲下繞啊繞，腳掌不小心踢到了緩緩爬行而過的蝸牛，蝸牛立刻全身縮起，將腹足藏進蝸牛殼裡。

　　天天對蝸牛說：「你也是像烏龜和野兔一樣，出來運動讓自己快樂的嗎？」蝸牛聽到聲音，這才小心翼翼的一點一點伸出腹足，慢慢探出頭恢復蝸牛的形狀說：「才不是呢！我是出來覓食的。」

天天說：「你不怕被踩到嗎？更何況你還是許多鳥和蛇的食物呢！」

蝸牛笑嘻嘻的說：「不怕不怕，小心點就好了！如果怕被踩就從此不出門，這樣不就會活活餓死嗎？所以我還是每天出來冒險，小心避開大家的腳，誰叫我長得這麼小。看，現在的我，不是好好的嗎？」

天天說：「你這麼勇於冒險，應該是因為你們蝸牛族每次產卵都至少一百個以上吧，哪像我們大貓熊要小心翼翼，不但生得少，又已經是瀕臨危險生存邊緣的族群了！」

　　蝸牛仍舊笑咪咪的回應天天：「我們生得多，可是我們折損率也高啊，所以更要好好的過每一分每一秒，學會欣賞生活中小小的樂趣，學會欣賞自己。像你這麼提心弔膽的，你們族群就會突然多生幾隻大貓熊，讓族群壯大嗎？而且你們雖然數量少，但壽命比我們蝸牛長得多了，至少可以活二、三十年，你要一直擔憂的活著嗎？還是快樂的活著呢？」

天天又接著抱怨：「你們雖然活得短，但至少大家都知道你們的名字叫『蝸牛』，不像我們一下被叫『大貓熊』，一下被叫『大熊貓』。大家連我們的名字都搞不清楚，好煩喔！」

　　蝸牛將腹足伸得更長，樂不可支的對天天說：「哈哈哈，這有什麼好煩的！雖然大家搞不清楚你們的名字，不是也愛了你們五千年嗎？」

蝸牛繼續說：「你們長得天生『萌』樣，大家一看到你們就覺得很療癒、很愉快！你不開心時拿鏡子照照自己，就可以很開心啦！」

　　天天走到河邊，看見水面映照出的自己，有著圓圓的頭、短短的尾巴，身體和頭部黑白分明的顏色，前掌除了五個帶爪的趾外，還有一個特別可愛的第六趾，天天心想：「天啊！我其實長得挺可愛的嘛，呵呵！」

蝸牛這時才慢慢爬到天天身邊說：「多欣賞自己就會快樂，像你說我動作慢，我也可以說我是堅持不懈啊！」「你想想看，你的家這麼大！自由自在的在山上生活，可以春天賞花海，夏天看山水，秋天觀雲霧，冬天踏傲雪呢！」

　　天天這才發現自己的家和蝸牛的家比起來，真的是天地寬廣！

天天突然又開始煩惱：「我生活得這麼好，卻還常生氣，有時拔自己的毛，有時亂摔東西，或者對爸媽大吼大叫，真是太不知惜福了！」

　　蝸牛聽完天天的煩惱，簡直要笑到岔氣：「回去好好改過，並且向爸媽道歉不就好了！這麼好的生活都能讓你過成這樣，真是服了你！」

蝸牛接著說：「你們大貓熊長期生活在密密麻麻的竹林裡，光線暗，障礙物又多，視力不是不太好嗎？記憶力好像也很短？但缺點也可以是優點啊！這樣應該可以讓你更容易忘記使你憤怒的事，原諒令你失望的人才對啊！哈哈哈！」「你看河邊的向日葵，每一棵都向著陽光生長，給點陽光就快樂！」「快樂是一種選擇，你永遠可以選擇每天都讓自己快樂。」

　　聽了蝸牛的話，看著自在生長、燦爛怒放的向日葵，天天覺得胸口鼓脹脹的，好像快樂就要溢出來一樣……

天天終於明白，原來快樂就是快樂，自己的快樂自己找。快樂的鑰匙在自己手中，只要我們想要自己快樂，沒人能奪得走！

天天決定要每天慢慢吃、好好睡、多多動，靜下心來愛自己、愛食物、愛家人、愛運動、愛周遭一切，學會珍惜發生在自己身上的每一件好事！

原來快樂這麼簡單，原來快樂就在自己身邊，快樂到處有，到處有快樂！

● 給教師及家長的話 ●

　　在特殊教育的工作領域裡，常會看到一些人只注意到自身的不完美，而無限放大自身痛苦，致使自己離快樂越來越遠的例子；也看到另外一群人總是活得生氣蓬勃，凡事學會自己動手做，並從做中得到快樂，或是每天樹立小目標，在實現理想中得到快樂的例子。這麼多年下來，我真心相信，擁抱快樂才能擁有好生活！快樂從來就不是一種奢求，而是一種選擇！而你永遠可以選擇每天都讓自己快樂。

　　對許多特殊需求孩子來說，他們拿到的可能是一手人生爛牌，但爛牌打到爛，其實很正常，若能在退無可退的情境下，承認現實、好好打人生的牌，漸次朝向好的目標靠近，周圍的人想必會發出豔羨的讚嘆！相對於一般正常孩子，一手好牌打到好是很正常的，但一手好牌若是不小心打糟了，懊惱之餘還得要承受各種壓力！所以有時我常逆向思考，覺得特殊需求孩子比較能擁有單純的快樂，就如同繪本中的大貓熊天天與蝸牛的想法對照。

　　現今教育界常提倡快樂學習，但我總覺得，真正的快樂必須讓人擁有愉悅感及意義感，也就是有意義的愉悅才是真正且自在的快樂，所以我比較相信成就學習，有成就感的學習才能真快樂！

　　對許多人而言，快樂可能來自於他們可以自我控制想要控制的事。例如：注意力缺陷過動症的孩子可以藉由醫療、運動、膳食或是行為改變技術控制自己的注意力和衝動思考，與大家共同坐在課堂學習，會是一種莫大的快樂！上班族解除壓力的方法或許不是帶著罪惡感去吃東西或睡覺以轉移注意力，而是把事情做完或是做好，進而得到別人真誠的讚美，那將會是一種無法取代的快樂！小小孩在自己小小的世界裡可以控制自己的手拿到想要的東西，自己獨立做完一件事，就可以讓他們樂不可支！

　　對許多人而言，快樂可能來自有足夠的人生智慧在對的時間做對的決定。正向思考的人生智慧是一種內在的價值觀，一般人並不會特別去注意自己的生活態度與思想結構，但生活態度與思想結構卻主宰了我們生活中的許多層面。處於順境的時候，大部分人是不會去想這些的，一旦身處在逆境中，才會知道正向思考的人生智慧的重要性，它能協助我們在對的時間做對的決定，在緊迫的關鍵點做出人生無悔的選擇，使我們的生活與他人產生有意義的連結。

對許多人而言，快樂可能來自能為自己做的決定負責。能自我負責會是一種很大的成就感，也是我們尊嚴感與自主性的來源。所以，決定預期的目標，逐步實行並自我負責就能得到快樂，可以讓我們從自身有需要、有興趣的事物，回歸到最原始、最簡單的方式，把這個事物做好。簡單的事情能做好就不簡單，平凡的事情能堅持就不平凡！

　　所以快樂是一種生活態度，快樂是一種選擇，身為家長或教師的我們，要記得快樂的生活態度是可以教導的，是會感染的！沒有快樂的爸媽，就不會有真正快樂的孩子；沒有快樂的教師，也不會有真正快樂的學生。讓我們協助孩子可以自我控制想要控制的事，而不是事事幫他完成；讓我們輔助孩子有足夠的人生智慧在對的時間做對的決定，而不是事事代替他做決定；支持孩子能為自己做的決定自我負責，而不是事事協助他善後。如果我們想要更快樂，那麼就在我們的生活中加入更多的愉悅感和意義感。而如果我們還沒想好怎麼做才能快樂，那麼至少讓我們如同繪本中的主角天天最後的體悟一樣，至少要每天慢慢吃、好好睡、多多動，靜下心來愛自己、愛食物、愛家人、愛運動、愛周遭一切，學會珍惜發生在自己身上的每一件好事！

Tian Tian's Pursuit of Happiness

Written by Ying-Ru Meng
Illustrated by Hui-Ting Lin
Translated by Arik Wu

Once upon a time, there was a giant panda named Tian Tian. He was always unhappy because the world just could not seem to get his species right. Sometimes he was called a bear, and other times, he was called a big raccoon. This really drove Tian Tian crazy and made him mad.

Tian Tian often wondered why the birth rate of pandas was so low. If it continued to be so, they would soon turn from living fossils to real fossils!

When he felt unhappy, he would pull his own hair, break things around him, and throw a tantrum at his parents. None of these things, however, would relieve his anger. Therefore, one day he decided to go for a walk outside.

He saw a black bear rubbing his back against a tree. The bear's eyes were partly closed due to the comfort that followed. "This feels great! This is wonderful!" he yelled. Beside the bear, there were several boars bathing joyfully in a mud pool. "It can't be any more comfortable!" the boars cried, each smiling from ear to ear.

Tian Tian did not understand why they looked so joyous, as if there was no trouble and sorrow in their lives. "Why do you look so happy?" he asked curiously.

"Because we are doing what we truly like!" the animals answered simultaneously.

"That's right! And remember, eating what you like also cheers you up! You see, I'm collecting nectar and pollen! This is not just for my own sake, but also for the reproduction of flowers. Helping others is also a great way to make you happy!" a honey bee suddenly joined the conversation.

Tian Tian then decided to emulate them. He found a rock that seemed rather comfortable, laid on the rock, and started rubbing his back against the rock slowly, while eating bamboos in an extremely casual manner. It was so enjoyable – he could not even spare a moment to clean up the bamboos that scattered his furry belly.

Tien Tien's presence, however, startled a turtle resting on the rock, and caused him to fall right to the ground, upside down. Tian Tian saw it, and quickly reached out a hand to help turn the turtle back up.

The turtle seemed rather grateful, and that reminded Tian Tian of what the bee had told him just a while ago. "Helping others is really a great way to make people happy," he repeated to himself. The fact that he could do what he liked, eat what he desired, and reach out to help those in need was truly making him more of a happy panda!

"Well, why is it that you don't just stay home and rest? You move so slowly, after all," Tian Tian asked the turtle. "I love doing exercise. It makes me happy. I've got to carry on walking no matter what," the turtle said.

"Exactly! Doing exercise is what makes me happy as well! Look how happy I am!" said a hare who happened to pass by. He was hopping up and down, looking genuinely delighted.

An image of him being very fit suddenly emerged in Tian Tian's mind. "I guess this is one of the good things about doing exercise regularly, right?" he said to himself. With this encouraging image in mind, he began hopping up and down like the hare and fast-walking round the turtle. "This will surely help get rid of the bamboos I just ate!" Tian Tian thought. A certain degree of happiness started to grow within him.

Tian Tian continued his stroll, under the bright, bright sun. The next thing that he came across was a snail slowly crawling somewhere. The moment the snail saw Tian Tian, he almost immediately withdrew into his shell. "Are you doing exercise, just like the turtle and the hare I met a moment ago?" Tian Tian asked out of curiosity. His voice calmed the snail down slightly, and then slowly, the snail crawled back out to meet Tian Tian. "Of course not! I'm just looking for something to eat!" the snail said.

"Aren't you afraid that someone might accidentally step on you? And, aren't you afraid of being eaten by birds and snakes?" Tian Tian asked, looking surprised.

"Of course not, there's no point in being afraid if I'm careful enough. If I'm always afraid of being stepped upon, I'm going to starve to death pretty soon. Every day, I do what I should do to survive, and avoid being killed by people's careless feet. I'm small, that's true, but who am I to blame? Look at me! At the end of the day, I'm still looking fabulous," the snail said, smiling.

"Well, I think the reason why you snails are so adventurous is because you lay more than 100 eggs every time you give birth. On the contrary, we pandas have to be very cautious every time we give birth to our newborns, since they are so few in number. Alas, I think we're already on the verge of extinction," Tian Tian could not help complaining.

The snail smiled in return, and said, "It's true that we have more newborns, but only a few of them survive at the end. So, it's really important for us to be able to appreciate every little thing in life and to love who we really are. It's pointless feeling worried all the time. It will definitely not help you pandas give birth to more newborns, will it? Also, though there're only a few of you, you pandas actually have longer lifespan than we do. Pandas can live up to 20 to 30 years! So are you going to spend time worrying about this and that, or are you going to spend time being happy?"

"You snails are relatively short-lived, I agree. However, at least people know what you are. You are SNAILS! As for pandas, sometimes we're called bears, and sometimes big raccoons. They just can't seem to get our species right! It annoys me to no end," Tian Tian continued to complain.

The snail stretched his head forward, seemingly amused by Tian Tian's words. "Well, there's no need to make a fuss about it. You see, it doesn't matter if they get it right or not, they still loved you for five thousand years, and are likely to continue doing so in the future!" he said.

"You see," the snail resumed, "You pandas are cute – in a way that people think it's rather comforting and joyful just by looking at you. Well, if you feel unhappy, just look at yourself in a mirror! It sure will make you happy."

Tian Tian then walked to the nearest river and observe his reflection in the water – He had a short tail, a balloon-shaped head, a large black-and-white body with a white face and black eye patches and ears, ten claws on the front paws, and, last but not least, two extra, thumb-resembling digits!

"Oh my! I think I'm kind of cute!" Tian Tian thought.

The snail crawled slowly to the side of Tian Tian, and said, "The more you are able to appreciate yourself, the happier you are. You see, you can definitely call me 'slow', but on the other hand, you can't deny that I'm 'persistent', right? Also, look at how large a habitat area you have! Living in mountains oozing such carefree vibes, you pandas get to do whatever you want! You get to see a sea of beautiful flowers in spring, enjoy the company of magnificent mountains and rivers in summer, observe the changing of clouds and fogs in fall, and take a stroll in the snow in winter!"

The snail's words reminded Tian Tian of just how fortunate it was to be a giant panda!

However, Tian Tian, was still a little worried. "I'm more fortunate than most animals already... yet I complain so much. I have even been pulling my hair, breaking things around me, throwing a tantrum at my parents... causing them so much trouble. I'm just so ungrateful," he said regretfully.

The snail burst into laughter immediately and said, "It's no big deal, really. Just go home and apologize to them, and make sure you will be good in the future. It's truly impressive how you are able to live such a great life as if it was a total disaster...."

"Wait a minute. If my memory serves me right, pandas are mostly near-sighted and don't have very good memory, right?" the snail continued. "That's probably because your species has long been living in shady bamboo forests where obstructions are common.... Well, that can be both a shortcoming and an advantage, don't you think? That means it's easier for you to forget about unpleasant experiences and to forgive those who have failed you. Look at those sunflowers along the riverbank. They always grow toward the sun. Just a little bit of sunlight will make their day. Well, my point is, happiness is a choice. You can always be happy if you wish to be so!"

Tian Tian saw those lovely and seemingly carefree sunflowers, and, all of a sudden, a great sense of happiness filled his heart.

He started to realize that the key to happiness lies within himself. "Happiness is a choice," he said to himself. "And once we make the decision to be happy, no one is able to make us unhappy!"

Tian Tian then decided to eat more slowly, sleep early, and do exercise regularly every day. He wished that he could love himself and his family more dearly, that he was better able to enjoy food and doing exercise, and that he could be more capable of appreciating everything around him. Most importantly, it was his ultimate wish that he could learn how to cherish every little good moment in life.

It turns out that the secret to happiness is really simple! Happiness is not something we need to take pains to discover. Happiness is everywhere, and everywhere there is happiness!